LUPE LOPEZ

READING ROCK STAR!

For Ms. Conley, Ms. Rivera, Mrs. Moore, and Mrs. Read,
who cultivate reading rock stars daily —eEC-T

To the Braun family—Julie, Jeff, Blair, and Hannah —PZM

For all those teachers who gave of themselves when it was the
hardest—and the most important. Thank you! —JC

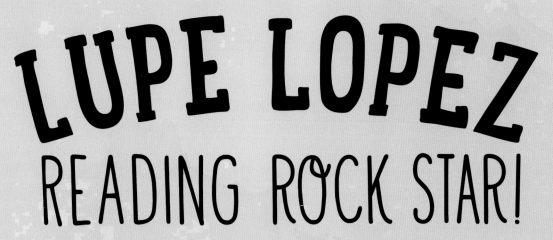

LUPE LOPEZ
READING ROCK STAR!

e.E. Charlton-Trujillo and Pat Zietlow Miller

illustrated by Joe Cepeda

CANDLEWICK PRESS

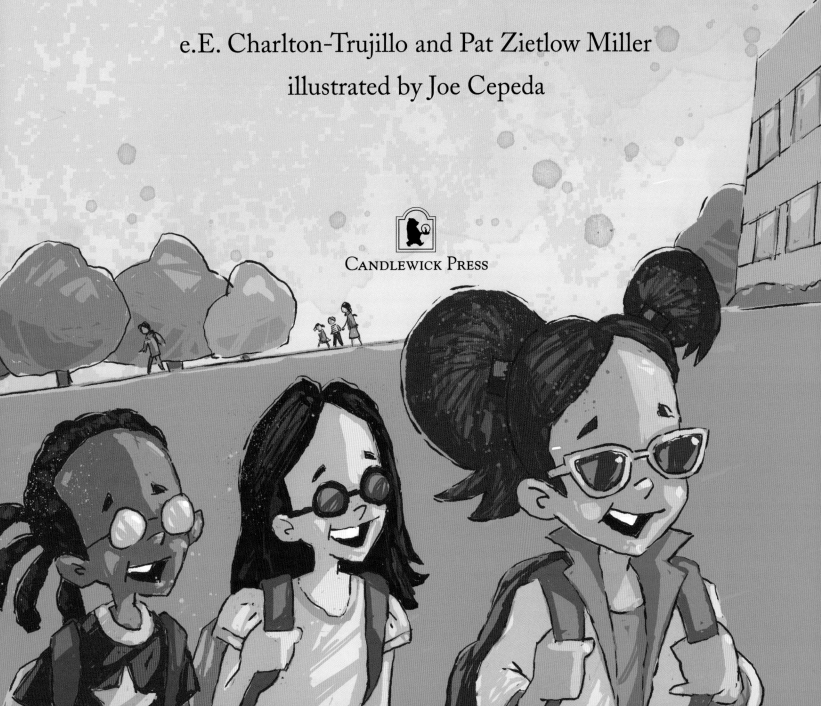

Lupe Lopez was famous at Hector P. Garcia Elementary School for being the first kid in kindergarten to EVER start a band. Which was kind of a big deal.

Now that she was in first grade, Lupe wanted a new kind of fame. Reading Rock Star fame.

Reading Rock Stars told the best stories, carried the coolest books, and scored the shiniest stars on the Wall of Fame.

Reading Wall of Fame!

Lupe rolled out a bookshelf beat as she strutted into class with bandmates Ana and Ruby.

¡RAN! ¡RATAPLÁN! ¡BOOM-TICA-BAM!

Lupe was ready to rock!
Lupe was ready to roll!

Lupe was ready to read!

She was about to start when Victor Valdez sat down in Group B.

Not Group A like Lupe, because *A* was for *AWESOME*, and Victor wasn't. The school year had barely started and he'd already snatched her sunglasses, laughed at her lunch box, and disrespected her drumsticks.

But Lupe was a rock star. Rock stars weren't bothered by kids like Victor. Especially with a shiny star on the line.

Lupe knew every word on her reading list. She'd practiced three times before school.

But when she looked at her book, the words looked . . . different.
They were lined up. One right after the other into . . . sentences?
Lupe stared at the sentences. They glared back.

Suddenly, it seemed like everyone in awesome Group A
was waiting for Lupe to read.

Which was kind of a big deal.

"Try to sound it out," said Ms. Moreno.

"*T-he*," Lupe tried. "*Th-e gi-gi . . .*"

"You can do it," Ruby whispered from Group B.

"Just like you practiced," added Ana.

"*The girl . . . ra . . . ra . . .*"

Victor laughed. "It's *ran*, Lupe. Everyone knows that."
"Victor . . ." said Ms. Moreno.

Lupe shrank.

No one should laugh at rock stars.
Especially Victor Valdez.
Just like that, Lupe was done reading.

During lunch, Lupe and the band practiced a new song.
Whenever Ana sang the chorus, Lupe drummed too fast.
    Ruby pointed to the lyrics.
    But Lupe couldn't *read* the lyrics. She'd always pretended.
Played it by ear.

Victor walked by and snatched Lupe's sunglasses.
"Look, I'm a rock star. Only I can't even read."

"I can read," Lupe said. "When I want."
Victor pointed at his juice box. "What's this say?"
"It says, 'Group A is for awesome readers. That's
why you're in Group B.'"

Victor laughed. "Group A is for
kids who *can't* read."

Lupe looked to the band.
"For real?" she asked.

"You won't be in Group A forever," said Ana.
"Definitely not," said Ruby.

But she was in Group A *now*. Maybe she *couldn't* read.

Lupe dropped the lyrics.

Left the lunchroom.

And quit the band.

It was the worst day a first-grader ever had at Hector P. Garcia Elementary.

The next day, Lupe wasn't ready to rock. Roll. Or read.
She even ignored her former bandmates as she walked into school.
She sat outside her reading group and stared at the floor.

"¿Qué pasa?" Ms. Moreno asked. "Don't you want your star?"

"You started a band in kindergarten, Lupe. You can do anything—
you just have to try," said Ms. Moreno. Then she whispered,
"I'll tell you a secret. Reading is like music."

Lupe shook her head.

Music was easy.

Reading was hard.

After school, Lupe waited outside a fruit cup stand.
She had no band. No fans. And no shiny star. But then . . .
the clerk called out:

"ELOTES! MANGONADAS!
CHAMOY APPLES! LIMONADAS!
FLAMING NACHOS. TWO FRUIT STICKS.
FRESADILLIES. BANANA SPLITS."

Lupe tapped her pencils to the beat of his voice.
Then she quietly sounded out words on the menu board.

To-day's Tast-y Tr-eats
E-lo-te
Man-go-na-da
Cha-moy . . . ap-ple and
Li-mo-na-da.

She tried again and again. Until the tap of her pencils matched the beat of the words.

Until the words sounded smoother.
Safer.
Then Lupe realized:

The beat had a sound.

That sound came from letters.
Those letters made words.
Words made sentences.
Sentences made songs.

And songs made— "Music!" Lupe shouted.

"Reading is like music! I just need to see the beat!"

As Lupe tapped the beat of every order,
she realized something else.
She needed to apologize to her friends.
And reunite the band.

So she did.

"It's OK," said Ruby.

"We've got your back," added Ana.

Just like that, the band was back together.

Lupe led the way to class.

Victor met her at the door.
"It's the Reading Rock Star."

Ruby stepped up.
"Do you know what a rock star is?"
"*I* do," said Ana. "It's someone who tries."

At their desks, the band air-drummed together:

¡RAN! ¡RATAPLÁN!

¡BOOM-TICA-BAM!

Lupe opened her book,
tapped her pencils, and . . .
"One word," said Ms. Moreno.
"After the next," said Lupe.
And with the beat of her pencils and the music
in her head, Lupe read.

Sometimes, she stammered.
Sometimes, she stumbled.
Sometimes, she even asked for help.

But when she was done, a star shimmered by her name.
And that was definitely a big deal!